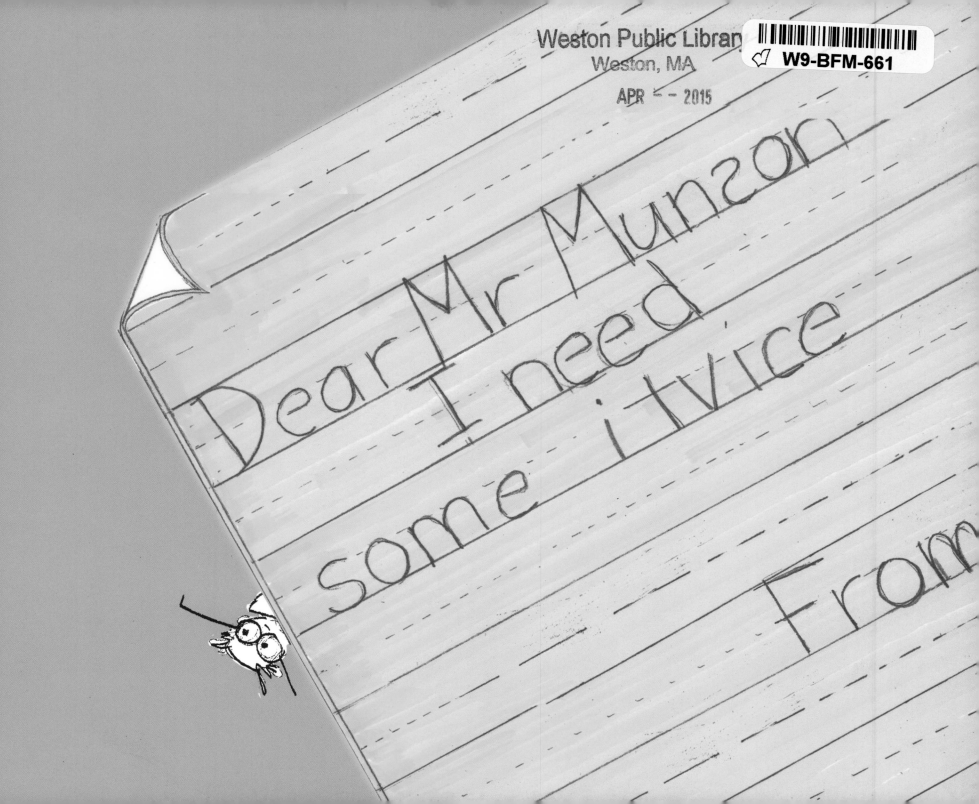

W9-BFM-661

Dear Mr Munson
I need
some itvice

From

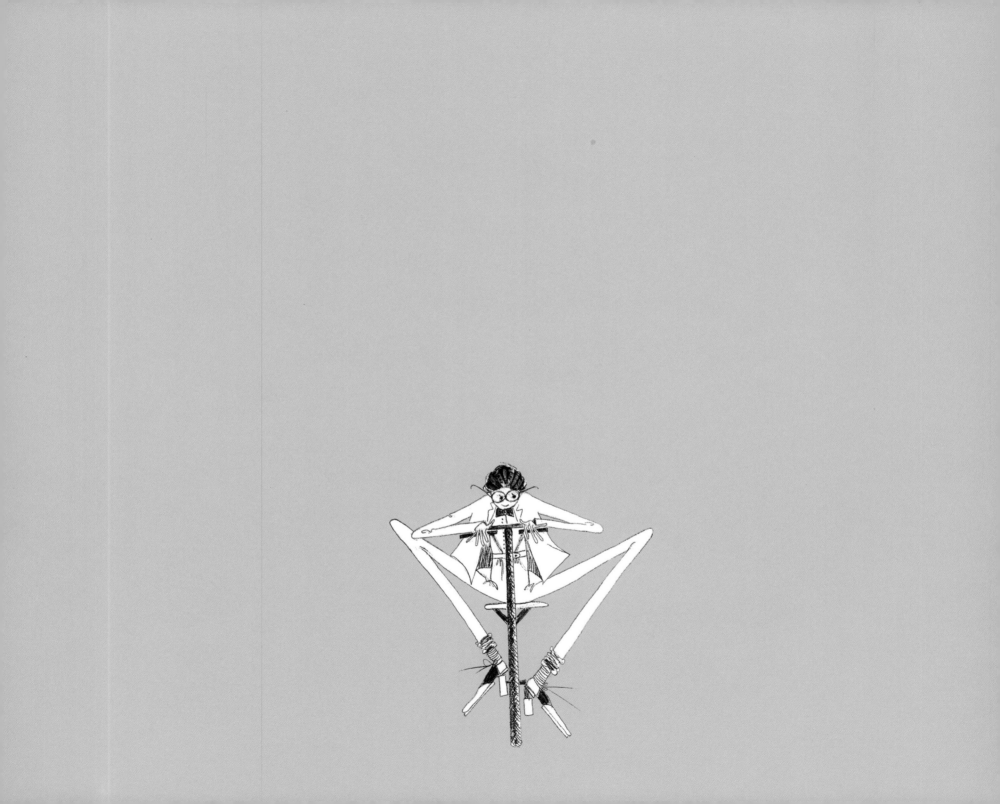

Mr. Munson's Advice on Bullying

Written by Nancy Nolan   Illustrated by Kathryn Scadden

BEAVER'S POND PRESS

Kathryn Scadden

ISBN: 978-1-59298-907-2

Library of Congress Catalog Number: 2014918954

Printed in the United States of America

Written by Nancy Nolan
Illustrations by Kathryn Scadden
Edited by Lily Coyle
Book design by Sara Weingartner
Design Assistant, Lisa Wanstead

Parent/teacher
J
302.34

BEAVER'S
POND
PRESS

Beaver's Pond Press, Inc.
7108 Ohms Lane
Edina, MN 55439-2129
(952) 829-8818
www.BeaversPondPress.com

www.mrmunsonsitvice.com

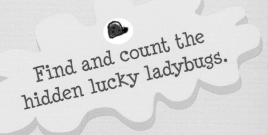

Find and count the hidden lucky ladybugs.

We dedicate this book
to those who
have ever been bullied,
have witnessed bullying,
or have been the bully.
We offer encouragement
for change.

Sometimes, it's hard being the new kid in school.

It's always hard being the new, shy kid who is bullied. That is what is happening to Stuart, and it's really starting to bother him.

3

So, when his teacher reminds the class that Mr. Munson, the guidance counselor at Pickle Pond Elementary School, will be visiting his class today, his ears perk up.

Pickle Pond Elementary School
RULES

Respect the rights of others.

Be kind to others.

Try to help others who are being bullied.

Include others who are left out.

Tell an adult if someone is being bullied.

Safety is your right!

Today, Mr. Munson is discussing bullying. He reminds the children that they always have the right to be safe.

"No one has the right to scare you."

"No one has the right to hurt your feelings."

"No one has the right to hurt you."

Cafeteria Worker Librarian Guidance Counselor Principal Vice Principal English Teacher Science Teacher Gym

Math Teacher English Teacher

Teacher Art Teacher Policeman Security Guard Bus Driver Mother Father Aunt Uncle

Counselor Crossing Guard School Administrator

Grandmother Grandfather Cousin Playground Monitor Nurse Math Teacher Fireman Office Aide Secretary Bus Driver Friend

"There's always a grown-up around who could help a child.
Just tell that grown-up you need help."

"Here are a few questions for you to think about," says Mr. Munson. "Please don't raise your hand with an answer; just answer in your heart. Have you ever seen anyone get bullied or teased in a hurtful way?

Have you ever been the one who was bullied?"

"This may be a harder question, have YOU ever been the one who has bullied another person?"

Stuart listens very carefully to this lesson.

Maybe Mr. Munson can help me.

So, Stuart goes to Mr. Munson's office for some "itvice."

"Kids make fun of my clothes."

"They make fun of my size."

"And they tease me because I'm not so good at math."

"I haven't bothered anyone. I'm friendly to all the kids. I just don't understand why they pick on me."

Mr. Munson listens to all that Stuart has to say, and it seems very clear that Stuart is trying to be a friend to his new classmates. Mr. Munson reminds Stuart about the lesson on bullying and some of the ideas that they had discussed in class.

"Did you try to ignore the bullies, Stuart?" asks Mr. Munson.
"Yes, I tried that for three days. It didn't work."

"Did you ask them to stop the bullying, Stuart?"

"Yes, and they just laughed at me."

16

"Did you try to stay with a group of friends, Stuart?"

"I remembered that idea, Mr. Munson, but I really haven't made many friends since I've started at this school."

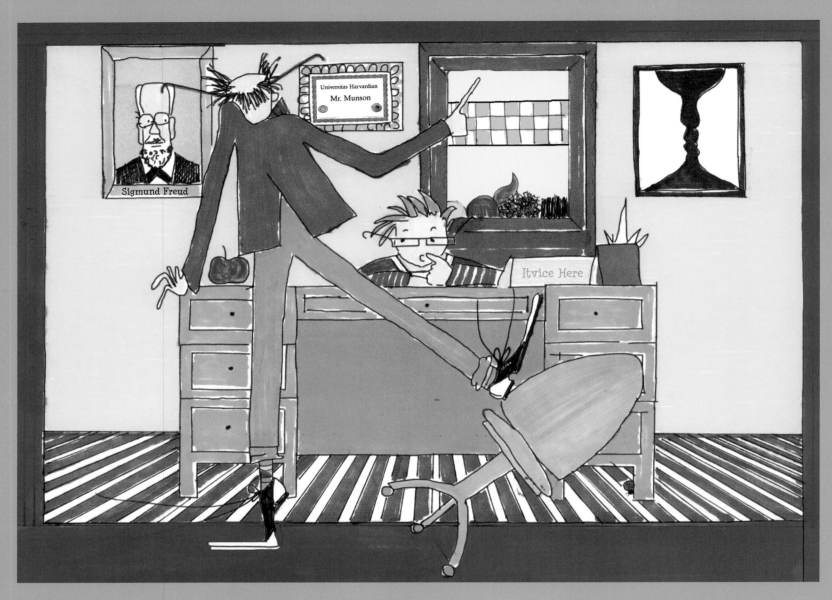

"Well," says Mr. Munson, "here's something else that you could try. The next time someone teases you, ask him or her a question."

"Ask someone a question? I don't understand how that could help."

"Let me explain," says Mr. Munson. "Whenever you ask someone a question, that person usually has to stop and think about answering the question. Sometimes that moment can change things. It might even give you more time to think about another question to ask or to even change the subject and start talking about something else."

"Do you think you could try that, Stuart? Oh, and one more thing to remember, using kindness and humor can change a situation. I don't mean making fun of the other person. I mean saying something really funny or telling a clever joke."

Stuart isn't sure about Mr. Munson's idea but agrees to think about it.

The next day when the class is in line for lunch, Carlos, the kid in front of Stuart, turns around and says to him, "you stink."

Stuart remembers Mr. Munson's "itvice" about asking a question, so he says, "well, what do I smell like?" Carlos looks quite surprised and pauses for a moment before he answers.

"Oh, you don't really stink. I was mad at that other kid over there, and I knew I could take it out on you."

"Oh," says Stuart with a long pause. "Hey, are you going to play baseball this spring?" Both boys start to talk about baseball as they wait in line for lunch.

They even sit down next to each other. Stuart listens as Carlos talks about playing baseball.

As they walk outside for recess, Carlos asks Stuart how many home runs he has ever hit. Stuart answers that he loves to play baseball but he has never hit a home run. "In fact, I kind of 'stink' at baseball!" They both laugh as they run onto the playground.

Mr. Munson sees Stuart in the library a few days later and asks how things are going. Stuart tells Mr. Munson what happened with Carlos in the lunch line. "I think I'm starting to understand a little more about bullying. I think I'm starting to feel a little more comfortable here at Pickle Pond. But I really think I need to learn a few more jokes. A kid has to know these kinds of things!"

Mr. Munson smiles. "Stop by my office sometime and tell me some of your best jokes, Stuart. We all need a good laugh every day."

Mr. Munson's Advice on Bullying:

1. Ignore the bully.
2. Walk away.
3. Ask the bully to stop.
4. Stay in a group.
5. Change the subject by asking a question.
6. Look confident.
7. Use humor.
8. Show kindness. (A bully never expects this.)
9. Tell a grown-up.

Know the Difference Between Tattling and Reporting:

Tattling is when:

    ...you tell on someone.

    ...the thing you're telling is NOT very serious.

    ...the reason you tattle is just to get someone in trouble.

Reporting is when:

    ...you tell on someone.

    ...the thing you're reporting is VERY serious.

    ...the reason you report is that someone needs help.

How many lucky ladybugs did you count? Answer hidden on the first two pages.